# THE RAIN CAME DOWN

## David Shannon

THE BLUE SKY PRESS

An Imprint of Scholastic Inc. · New York

FOR BONNIE

THE BLUE SKY PRESS

Text and illustrations copyright © 2000 by David Shannon
All rights reserved.
No part of this publication may be reproduced, stored
in a retrieval system, or transmitted in any form or by any
means, electronic, mechanical, photocopying, recording,
or otherwise, without written permission of the publisher.
For information regarding permission,
please write to: Permissions Department,
Scholastic Inc., 557 Broadway, New York, New York 10012.
SCHOLASSTIC, THE BLUE SKY PRESS, and associated logos are
trademarks and/or registered trademarks of Scholastic Inc.
Library of Congress catalog card number: 99-086363
ISBN 978-0-439-05021-0
20 19 18 17 16 15 14               13 14 15 16/0
Printed in Malaysia   108
First printing, October 2000

**O**n Saturday morning, the rain came down.
It made the chickens squawk.

The cat yowled at the chickens, and the dog barked at the cat.

And still, the rain came down.

The man yelled at the dog and woke up the baby.
"Stop all that yelling!" shouted the man's wife.

The dog barked louder.
And still, the rain came down.

A policeman heard the noise
and stopped to see what was wrong.

His car was blocking traffic, and half a block away,
a woman squirmed in the back of a taxi.

"Hurry up, or I'll miss my plane!" she told the taxi driver.
So he started honking his horn.

The truck driver in front of him got mad and started honking back.
"I have tomatoes to deliver!" he shouted.

The ice-cream man heard the honking
and turned up the music on his van.

"Jingle-a-jingle," went his music.
"Slappa-de-slap," went his windshield wipers.
And still, the rain came down.

The owner of the beauty parlor came out to see what all
the fuss was about. She bumped into the barber coming out
of his barbershop, and they began to argue.

Up on his ladder, the painter grumbled, "I can't paint in the rain." He started to climb down and bonked the barber in the head with his can of paint. Now, all three of them were arguing.

Next, the baker stepped out of his bakery. "My roof is leaking, and my cakes are getting wet!" he moaned. He opened his umbrella and poked the pizza man in the nose. So they joined in the bickering, too.

A boy ran by, chasing a small boat down the stream in the gutter.

He splashed a little girl, and she began to cry.

And still, the rain came down.

The grocery man stomped out onto the sidewalk and yelled, "Where is that delivery truck? I need my tomatoes!" He ran into a lady coming out of the clothing store and knocked her boxes into his fruit stand.

Oranges, apples, and lemons bounced down the sidewalk.
And still, the rain came down.

The policeman walked back to his car. "What is all this ruckus about?"
he asked. The whole block was honking, yelling, bickering, and barking.

And then . . .

. . . the rain stopped!

And so did the noise. The sun came out,
and the air smelled fresh and sweet. Everything shimmered,
and a rainbow stretched across the rooftops.

"It's much too nice a day to be arguing!" said the baker.
"I have cakes to bake!"
"And I have pizzas to make!" said the pizza man.

"I could use a shave while my building dries,"
said the painter to the barber.
Then they went inside.

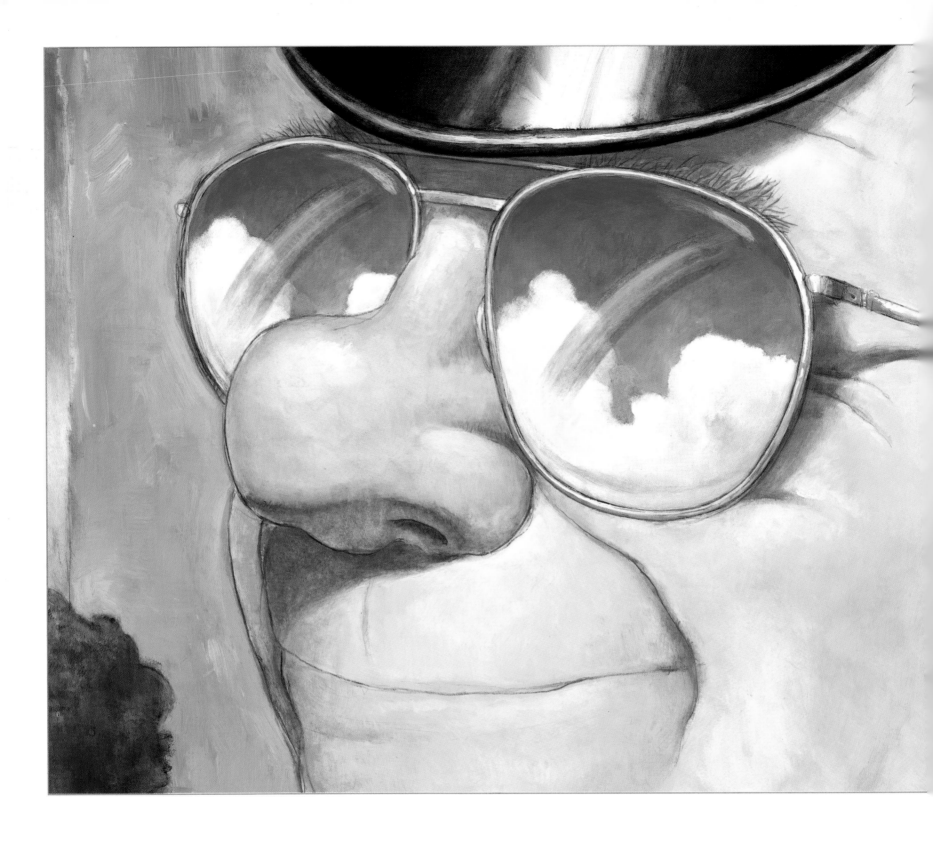

The policeman said, "Everything looks A-OK here to me."

And he drove off in his car.

The woman in the taxi decided she had time to have her hair done before her trip, and she went into the beauty parlor.

So the lady with the boxes got into the taxi and went home.

The truck driver told the grocer, "I have your tomatoes."
"Wonderful!" said the grocer. "But first,
I have to pick up this fruit."

The little girl and boy helped him, so he bought them ice-cream cones. And the ice-cream man gave them each an extra scoop, because it was such a nice day.

Then, the man, his wife, and their baby had a picnic together
in the backyard, while the dog, the cat, and the chickens
slept in the warm afternoon sun.